Farmyard Beat

by
Lindsey Craig

illustrations by
Marc Brown

Alfred A. Knopf

New York

For my amazing family
—L.C.

For our lovely dancing Isabella
—M.B.

THIS IS A BORZOI BOOK PUBLISHED BY ALFRED A. KNOPF

Text copyright © 2011 by Lindsey Craig
Jacket art and interior illustrations copyright © 2011 by Marc Brown

All rights reserved. Published in the United States
by Alfred A. Knopf, an imprint of Random House Children's Books,
a division of Random House, Inc., New York.

Knopf, Borzoi Books, and the colophon are registered
trademarks of Random House, Inc.

Visit us on the Web! www.randomhouse.com/kids

Educators and librarians, for a variety of teaching tools,
visit us at www.randomhouse.com/teachers

Library of Congress Cataloging-in-Publication Data
Craig, Lindsey.
Farmyard beat / by Lindsey Craig ; illustrations by Marc Brown.
p. cm.
Summary: The sounds of the farm animals create a lively beat that keeps
Farmer Sue, the chicks, sheep, and other farm animals awake.
ISBN 978-0-375-86455-1 (trade) — ISBN 978-0-375-96455-8 (lib. bdg.)
[1. Stories in rhyme. 2. Domestic animals—Fiction. 3. Bedtime—Fiction.]
I. Brown, Marc Tolon, ill. II. Title.
PZ8.3.C84367Far 2011   [E]—dc22   2010016123

The text of this book is set in 40-point and 60-point Arthur.
The illustrations in this book were created using hand-painted papers and a
collage technique that focused on cutting the paper into primary shapes.

MANUFACTURED IN CHINA
June 2011
10 9 8 7 6 5 4 3 2 1

First Edition

Peep-peep-peep!

Chicks can't sleep. Chicks can't sleep.
Chicks can't sleep
'cause they got that beat!

Peep! Peep! Peep-peep-peep!

Peep! Peep! Peep-peep-peep!

All that peeping wakes up . . . .

Sheep!
Sheep can't sleep.
Sheep can't sleep.
Sheep can't sleep
'cause they got that beat.

TAT! TAT! Tattity-tat-tat!

TAT! TAT! Tattity-tat-tat!

All that racket wakes up . . .

Cat!
Cat can't sleep.
Cat can't sleep.
Cat can't sleep
'cause she's got that beat.

Puuurrrrr! Mee-ooow!

Puuurrrrr! Mee-ooow!

All that racket wakes up . . .

Cow!
Cows can't sleep.
Cows can't sleep.
Cows can't sleep
'cause they got that beat

SWISH! CLANK! Swish-swish! Clank!

SWISH! CLANK! Swish-swish! Clank!

All that racket wakes Ol' . . .

Hank!
Hank can't sleep.
Hank can't sleep.
Hank can't sleep
'cause he's got that beat.

Woof! How-WOOOOO!

Woof! How-WOOOOO!

All that racket wakes up . . .

Shhh! Shhh!
Look who's coming!

FARMER SUE!!!

Sue can't sleep.

Sue can't sleep.

Sue can't sleep

'cause she's heard that beat.

Sue looks here! Sue looks there!

"No one here or anywhere!"

With a y-a-w-n, she thinks she'll go to sleep

when . . .

Peep! Peep!
Peep-peep-peep!
Chicks can't help it.
They got that beat!
Then . . .

TAT! TAT! Tattity-tat-tat!

Puuurrrr! Mee-ooow!

SWISH! CLANK! Swish-swish! Clank!

Woof! How-WOOOOO!

WHOOO? WHOOO?

JIG! JIG! A-jiggity-jig!

Everyone's dancing to that beat.

T-I-L-L . . .

. . . they fall in a heap!

Asleep!

Cock-a-doodle-doo!
I've got that beat!